HEATHER PECK has had
she was both farmer and agr
sheep and alpacas, reared c
the UK in international negotiations, spec
response from Chernobyl to bird flu, managed controls over pesticides and GM crops, saw legislation through parliament and got paid to eat KitKats while on secondment to Rowntree.

In the second half Peck chaired an NHS Trust, worked on animal welfare, sailed a boat on the Norfolk Broads, volunteered in Citizens Advice and the Witness Service and vaccinated humans against Covid. Two golden threads have run through everything, her fascination with words and her Gran's wise advice: 'You can do anything if you try hard enough.'

She writes about the countryside and the animals she loves, the industry (farming) she holds in deepest respect, and issues she is passionate about.

Peck's main protagonist has grown with each story and his life has changed in ways she couldn't have predicted at the start. She'd like to meet him. www.heatherpeckauthor.com.

Other books by Heather Peck

DCI GREG GELDARD SERIES

Secret Places
*Glass Arrows**
Fires of Hate

***shortlisted for the East Anglian Book Awards prize for fiction 2021**

DEATH
ON THE
RHINE

A DCI GREG GELDARD NOVELLA

Heather
Peck

Published in 2022 by Ormesby Publishing

ISBN 978-1-91576-902-2 (paperback)
ISBN 978-1-91576-903-9 (ebook)

British Library Cataloguing in Publication Data
A CIP catalogue record for this book is available from the British Library

Page design and typesetting by SilverWood Books
www.silverwoodbooks.co.uk

To Gary

…still loving and still laughing…

Acknowledgements

My thanks, yet again, to Geoff Dodgson and Alison Tayler for meticulous comments on an earlier draft.

Flash Forward

The dark air was moving softly, creating small eddies in the invisible flow. Looking over the side, he saw the lights from numerous cabins reflected in the river water below. He turned, to make a comment, and those yellow, moving reflections were the last thing he saw, before the explosion of stars and the cold embrace.

Chapter 1

It was the regular event – a quick pint and some supper at their favourite hostelry, the King's Arms. Sometimes they were joined by their other halves, but today just the three men had made it. They shared a subtle similarity of looks, although unrelated and originating in different parts of England. Short-haired, clean shaven and well-muscled with a look, above all else, of men who could cope in a crisis; if you didn't know better, you might think 'ex-military'. In fact, two were serving police officers and the third, Ben, had divided his career between nursing and the police before becoming a first responder.

Drinks in front of them and food ordered, they settled in for a long evening of gossip and news. Jim and Greg were unwinding after a long and difficult case involving people smuggling and multiple deaths. Ben was gearing up to a tricky announcement. He knew he'd have nothing but mickey-taking when he admitted to his holiday plans. He was right. Jim spluttered his beer all over the King's Arms' bar and Greg roared with laughter.

'A cruise? A river cruise,' choked Jim. 'Oh, come on, Ben. They're for retired old dears with lots of money and mobility problems.'

'Rubbish,' said Ben. 'All the paperwork keeps stressing how fit we need to be. And anyway,' he added with an afterthought that rather spoiled his argument, 'I am retired. Well – sort of. And Paula will be in weeks. I don't see what's so funny,' he said to Greg, with mild irritation.

'That's because you're not looking at your face,' replied Greg. 'I've never seen anyone announce they're taking a luxury holiday with less enthusiasm. You look as though you've been condemned to a month at Her Majesty's pleasure rather than ten days viewing the glorious sights of the Moselle and Upper Rhine from the luxury of your private balcony, a glass of champagne in your hand.'

'Have you been reading the brochure?' Ben demanded. 'Or do you write them in your spare time?'

'My parents went on one,' admitted Greg. 'They thought it was great. They loved the touring without having to keep packing and unpacking. And they said the food was amazing too.'

'I just don't see you hobnobbing with all those retired insurance salesmen and ex-army types,' said Jim, waving at the bar for refills. 'Tours of the wartime cemeteries are bound to be stuffed full of old army types. How did you afford it anyway?' he asked rudely. 'On a copper's pension?'

'The wife's parents,' replied Ben. 'It's a present for our wedding anniversary. They said it'd be like a second honeymoon.'

'And will it?' asked Jim with the beginnings of another burst of laughter. 'I thought your first was in a tent in Pembrokeshire.'

'It was,' said Ben. 'It rained for a week, the tent leaked and the farm dog stole the sausages off our camping-gas ring. Nothing could be as bad as that.'

A month later he had cause to remember that comment, and regret it.

It had started well enough. The early morning limousine transfer, provided free of charge by the cruise company, had been prompt and efficient, albeit the vehicle itself was more tatty taxi than luxury limo. The driver whisked them and their cases to Norwich airport, reminded them to pay their airport tax and left them to check their baggage in. The early morning airport was surprisingly busy.

'I thought this was supposed to be a quiet time,' muttered Paula. 'Where've this lot come from?' A long queue of families in colourful hot weather clothing snaked round the departures hall. 'Do we really have to queue up behind all these? I thought we were on a small plane.'

'That's right,' said Ben. 'One of those where they ask for volunteers to help wind up the elastic band. At least, that's how Greg described it. No, look. This crowd's going to Marbella. This is our queue,' he said with some relief, pointing to two couples standing by a sign that said 'Amsterdam'. As they joined the mini queue one couple moved to the desk and two more folk came to stand behind Ben and Paula.

'Going to Amsterdam?' asked the lean gentleman carrying a backpack with a familiar-looking luggage tag.

'That's right,' replied Ben again, as Paula was struggling with the paperwork. 'Are you on a cruise?' he asked. 'I see you have the same luggage tags as us.'

'Amsterdam to the Moselle and the Upper Rhine?' replied the man. And as Ben nodded, he said, 'Pleased to meet you. I'm Alec and this is Sue.'

'Ben and Paula,' said Ben in reply. Then, as the lady at the desk waved them forward, he added, 'See you later, I'm sure.'

The KLM flight was uneventful and short. So short indeed, that the in-cabin refreshments consisted of a bottle of water and what the packaging claimed was a Dutch-style biscuit, more or less thrown at them by the fast-moving air hostess. Ben regarded his biscuit dubiously and found himself insufficiently hungry to justify tackling the child-proof plastic. Next to him Paula took a bite, grimaced and hid the rest of it behind the instructions on what to do when they came down in the sea. Taking refuge in her battered copy of *All Quiet on the Western Front*, she asked, 'What time is it now in the Netherlands?' Ben checked his watch.

'They're one hour ahead, so it's just after eight,' he replied. 'We should be at the boat in time for lunch.'

At Schiphol they walked for what seemed like miles and, following their instructions, arrived at a meeting point near a Burger King outlet. There were lots of tour reps milling around holding up boards, some with names on, others just with logos. There was none with their name and none with the River Jewels logo either. Gradually, as other groups gathered, were greeted and departed, a small conglomeration of couples with River Jewels Cruises emblazoned on their luggage tags gradually accumulated. Everyone exchanged polite greetings, asked if anyone had seen their rep (no one had) and after a moment or two exchanged first names. Ben noted they had now been joined by a Gwyn and Gwen as well as Alec and Sue, Jeremy and Chris, and Richard. He also noted that Greg had been right. They were all older than Paula and him, and although most looked relatively fit, at least two seemed to be struggling with all the standing around and Gwen was already complaining about her knees. He made a mental note to keep quiet about his NHS links just as he heard Paula say, 'I'm a retired teacher, but Ben here still works as an NHS first responder.'

He sighed, and steeled himself to ten days alternately defending the NHS and avoiding being trapped into diagnosis of everything from heart murmurs to what, on the basis of past experience, he was sure his fellow guests would refer to as 'prostrate' cancer.

Conversation among the waiting group was fitful. A pattern soon emerged. Whatever the subject matter – ships, planes, war memorials, war – it soon became the victim of a monologue from Richard, making his reluctant interlocutors the gift of his lengthy opinions.

Just as patience was beginning to run out, a breathless blonde galloped into the arrivals hall waving a River Jewels banner and a furled umbrella.

'Sorry, folks,' she gasped. 'Our minibus was delayed, but it's here now. If I can just tick you all off my list, we'll get you to the ship soonest.'

With luggage stacked in the back, and ten passengers plus driver, the minibus was crammed to bursting point.

'Well, this is cosy, isn't it?' bubbled the blonde, who gave her name as Tess and her role as cruise director. 'And how brill that you all had time to get to know each other at the airport before we arrived.' She flashed another smile around. Gwyn from Cardiff cleared his throat.

'Well, it might have been better if we'd been met on time,' he said, but the second half of his sentence was drowned under Tess's relentlessly cheerful account of the other guests, those already on board and those still awaited. Gwyn was still looking grumpy as the minibus arrived at the destination, a long and rain-lashed stretch of quay with two river cruisers tied up nearby, one alongside the other.

'Our boat's the outer one,' explained Tess. 'Just identify your luggage as it comes off the minibus, then go aboard and cross the deck of the first boat to reach the *Diamond*. That's right,' she chivvied them, 'just pick out your cases… But first, let's give it up for our driver, Jacob.' Her audience stared at her blankly, then, as she demonstrated her meaning by bringing her hands together, a thin, scattered applause broke out.

Ben, in common with most of the male half of the assembled company, went over to the cases standing in the rain, and pointed out his and Paula's to the soaked crew members in logoed polo shirts and black trousers. To his surprise he found Gwen at his elbow, looking out her and Gwyn's bags while Gwyn himself took refuge aboard the river cruiser without a backward glance.

'Here,' said Ben, 'show me which are yours and I'll make sure they're collected.'

'That's very kind of you,' said Gwen. 'Gwyn's rheumatics play up something rotten if he gets wet.'

'No problem,' said Ben, and he watched as she turned and limped up the gangway.

'Not worse than yours I'd guess,' he muttered, and pointed out the two battered brown cases to the crew before going aboard himself.

The ship's lounge was comfortable, even luxurious, with ample squashy sofas and a bar at one end.

'The staff will take your orders for drinks,' said Tess, 'and at twelve they'll serve a buffet lunch. As soon as your cabins are ready you'll be taken to them, and the ship sails at 5pm. I'll be giving you your first port briefing at 5.30 and then dinner will be served on the deck below this one at 7pm. There's just the one sitting, so do please be there in time. In the meantime, welcome aboard the *River Diamond* and enjoy your lunch.'

Ben sat down with Paula and used his clean hankie to wipe some of the rain from his face. 'Have you ordered drinks?' he asked.

'Yes. I asked for a beer for you. Is that OK?'

'Yes, lovely, thanks.' He watched as Gwen took Gwyn's drink back to the bar, then came back with a substitute.

'You're frowning,' said Paula. 'What's bothering you?'

'Oh, nothing,' said Ben. 'At least, I'll tell you when we go down to our cabin.'

But it wasn't until after lunch that they were given the key card for their cabin, and he forgot what he'd been going to say.

The theme of relentless good cheer continued at Tess's first briefing. She explained the ship would sail a little later than planned as two guests had experienced problems with their flight connections and would only be joining the ship during dinner.

'But I'm sure you'll give them a big welcome,' she trilled, 'and the later sailing means that you early risers will see the *Diamond* going through some locks tomorrow morning.

'Now, I'm just going to introduce Captain Maurice, our hotel manager, Carl, and my assistant here, Felix. So let's give it up for Captain Maurice and his crew. You'll be seeing more of him at the safety briefing at 1100 tomorrow.'

Most of the passengers looked around bewildered, until the experienced few from the minibus hissed, 'She means clap,' and set the example.

Ben and Paula found themselves next to Gwen and Gwyn at dinner, with empty seats at the end of their six-seat table. It seemed the guests more experienced in the ways of cruises and passengers had made a swift assessment of the likely entertainment value of the pair from Cardiff and opted to sit elsewhere. Ben intercepted a couple of sympathetic glances from Alec and Sue, now resplendent, respectively, in grey linen suit and grey dress shimmering with bugle beads. Ben wondered if his blue open-necked shirt and chinos were a bit downmarket, but a glance at his wife in cream silk shirt and slacks reassured him that at least one of them was up to par.

'You look lovely, darling,' he said to her, raising his glass in a toast. 'To a second honeymoon.' She clinked her glass with his, but they were both distracted by Gwyn reaching over the table to take the menu from Gwen.

'I'll order for you, dear,' he said, and she meekly handed over the menu.

‘I’d thought of having the trout,’ she began, but Gwyn overrode her.

‘No certainly not,’ he said. ‘Bound to upset you. My wife will have the tomato soup and the steak. No sauce,’ he said to the waiter.

At that moment they were interrupted by a voice to their left.

‘Mind if we join you?’ it said. ‘Sorry we’re late. Our flight connection didn’t, if you see what I mean, and we got diverted via Paris. Still. Here now, that’s the main thing.’ A bearded Australian sat down next to Paula and a highlighted blonde in her sixties next to Ben.

‘Welcome,’ said Ben, as a waiter handed them menus. ‘No problem at all. We’ve only just ordered.’

‘You must be shattered,’ sympathised Paula. ‘Have you just arrived from Australia?’

‘No, thank God,’ said the beard. ‘I’m Blake, by the way, and this is my wife, Pen. We’ve been in Italy for a week. It was the connection in Rome that got fouled up. No worries. We’re here now.

‘Mine’s a beer,’ he said to the waiter, ‘and make it a big one. Or bring two. It’s been a stressful day.’

Tess appeared suddenly over his shoulder.

‘Everything all rightie?’ she asked. Then, without waiting for a reply: ‘That’s good. Your baggage’s been taken down to your cabin, so you’re all set now. See you at the safety briefing in the morning. Don’t be late for that!’ And she dashed away distributing smiles to left and right. Blake watched her go.

‘Do you think the smile switches off when she gets through the door?’ he asked.

Chapter 2

The highlight of the morning's safety briefing, as Ben later reported it to Greg, was the advice on what to do in the event of a sinking.

'Go upstairs,' recommended Captain Maurice, without the trace of a smile. 'The river is shallower than the *Diamond*. In the very unlikely event of a sinking,' he looked round the assembled guests, 'go up to the top deck and wait there.'

Further words on how to put on life jackets attracted about as much attention as the same advice on a plane; more advice about not sticking your head over the parapet when going under low bridges, and not leaning from their balconies while going through a lock, and the captain disappeared, still without a smile. Tess was a fraction late with her plea that they 'give it up once more for the captain' and the applause followed him down the stairs.

'Not a people person,' remarked Pen over their shoulders.

'Mind if we join you? Two coffees, please,' she said to the steward, then to Ben and Paula, 'Are you on a trip today?'

'Yes. Ypres and Passchendaele. You?'

'The same. We thought we'd get the depressing bit over at the beginning and then hit the vineyards for the second half of the trip.'

'Us too,' said Ben with a grin. 'But is it depressing? I think it's sad, and moving, but I wouldn't have said depressing.'

'It's the thought that everyone was certain they were in the right that depresses me,' said Blake, taking a seat with a heavy sigh. 'If I ever get out of this sofa it'll be a miracle,' he added. 'What're you reading?' he asked Paula, then as she showed him the cover of *All Quiet on the Western Front* said, 'You know what I mean if you're reading that.'

'What is it?' asked Pen. 'I don't think I know that book.'

'It's the First World War from the German perspective,' replied Paula, and Blake said, 'It's famous, Pen. I'm amazed you haven't read it. It illustrates my meaning exactly. The attitudes of the soldiers on both sides were pretty similar. And if that's still true today, which I think it is, we could end up in the same boat as our grandfathers. That's why I think the wartime cemeteries are depressing. It's the thought there could be more.'

'Well, you're cheerful and no mistake,' exclaimed Pen. 'Let's change the subject before we're all crying in our beer. Did I hear something about you two being on a second honeymoon?'

'That got round quickly,' exclaimed Ben, and Paula asked, 'Where did you hear that?'

'Overheard Teflon Tess telling her assistant bloke that you'd be a good pair to nobble for the Mr & Mrs game they've got planned for one evening.'

Ben looked thoroughly alarmed. 'No way,' he said, 'I'd rather jump overboard,' while Paula laughed.

'We'd lose anyway,' she said. 'I bet he can't even name my eye colour let alone my favourite piece of music.'

'Grey, and "Leaving on a Jet Plane",' said Ben triumphantly.

'I suppose one out of two isn't bad,' said Paula.

'OK then, what about mine?' demanded Ben.

'Brown and either "When All Is Said and Done" or "Only You".'

'Oh,' said Ben, disconcerted. 'Oh, right.'

Blake and Pen were laughing, and laughed some more as Ben described their first honeymoon, rain and sausage theft included.

'And he hasn't mentioned the worst bit,' added Paula. 'The airbed deflated every night.'

They were interrupted by the arrival of Gwen and Gwyn. Gwyn settled himself in an armchair nearby with a sigh which mirrored Blake's and said, 'Coffee please, dear. You know how I like it.' Gwen popped her newspaper down on the table and trotted off to the coffee machine in the corner.

'The waiters are happy to bring it over if you ask them,' remarked Ben.

'No thanks,' said Gwyn. 'Gwen knows how I like it.'

Gwen limped back with two cups of coffee and put them down on the table in front of Gwyn.

'No biscuits!' he exclaimed, and Gwen obediently went back for a plate of biscuits. Just as she sat down, Gwyn took a sip of his coffee, exclaimed in horror and slammed it back into the saucer. 'Gwen, it's undrinkable. So bitter. It needs more milk and sugar.'

'Oh, sorry, Gwyn,' she said and heaved herself out of her chair again. Ben and Paula exchanged looks and Ben said, 'Allow me,' but was interrupted by Gwen.

'No, it's fine,' she said. 'I know how he likes it, see.' And returned again to the coffee corner.

The conversation had languished. In an attempt to resurrect it, Pen asked, 'Are you coming on the wartime memorials trip?' Gwen opened her mouth but Gwyn spoke over her.

'I'm afraid we're not up to that,' he said, 'my hip, see. I'd be a martyr to it if I did too much.'

'I'd have liked to give it a go,' said Gwen. 'I think I could pace myself.'

'It's not too late,' said Pen, and Paula added, 'And we could keep an eye out for you. Gwyn would be fine here on the ship, wouldn't you?' She turned to Gwyn with a slightly martial look in her eye, but both the Rees's were shaking their heads.

'No. Thank you, but no,' said Gwyn. 'We'll just have a quiet potter along the bank here, then lunch on board.' Pen shrugged.

'Well, if you're sure,' she said. 'Come on, Blake. Let's get ready for the coach.'

As they joined the small queue for the gangplank, the more active passengers were already gathering around the collection of ship's bikes, ready for their cycling tour.

'Coach A for the Ypres tour, and Coach B for the walking tour of Antwerp,' said Tess, over and over as the gaggle of passengers checked the personal barcodes on their name tags at the readers by the gangplank and left the ship.

'Don't forget to check out, or we might leave without you,' said Felix. 'And don't forget to check in on your return or we'll be sending out search parties.'

A stiff breeze was blowing down the river and Paula only just caught her sun hat as it made a convulsive leap for freedom.

'Careful,' said Gwen behind her. 'You need a hat pin, like me.' She demonstrated the impregnability of her hat by a tug at its brim. Sure enough, it remained immoveable.

'Trouble is, I'd need the bun to skewer it to as well,' replied the bobbed Paula as they moved up to the river bank.

On Coach A, Ben and Paula found themselves sitting in front of Blake and Pen, and alongside Alec and Sue. The coach was almost full when their local guide, a short, dapper man wearing shorts and a straw hat, went down the aisle to complete his head count.

'OK,' he said. 'Welcome *Diamond* passengers. I'm Herman, your guide today for the war memorials at Ypres and Passchendaele, or Iepers as we call the town. You will see, as we drive along, that road signs commonly list village names in two spellings, both Flemish and French, as both languages are spoken here.'

'Just like Wales' muttered Ben to Paula, undercover of the continuing story of the history of Ypres from Roman times to the First World War. After a short while, Ben found his attention drifting to the scenes outside the bus windows. He noticed the town planning seemed more imaginative than in Britain, with an apparent rule that in any terrace of houses, the styles of roofs, windows, doors and fascia all had to vary from one house to the next. It made for a delightfully eclectic street scene and he was just about to draw Paula's attention to it when he was struck by a comment from the guide.

'Notice the trees,' he was declaiming. 'All the trees you see in this area are no more than 100 years old, because, of course, everything was destroyed in the First Great War.'

Thinking about it, and of the photos he'd seen of the battlefields, it was an obvious fact. But more than anything else it brought home to Ben the extent of the devastation inflicted. Blake leaned round and interrupted his reflections.

'What d'you think about that Gwyn bloke?' he asked. 'What a bully, eh? Poor woman.'

Exercising a modicum of tact, Ben nodded and agreed, conscious of Alec listening in from the seat opposite.

'I suppose all couples have their own way of doing things,' he said. Blake leaned back with a grunt and Paula looked at Ben.

'That's not what you really think, is it?' she whispered.

'No,' he said quietly. 'If I was on duty I'd be thinking about reporting safeguarding concerns. But I'm not, so…' He shrugged.

The guide interrupted his historical monologue to give them all a break, and Ben found himself dozing. The next time he opened his eyes, they were arriving at Tyne Cot cemetery. The gently curving rows of white headstones and red rose bushes induced an instant calm, and all the passengers dispersed to wander among the graves.

'Why do some have small piles of pebbles on them?' asked Ben of the person next to him, who turned out to be Alec.

'I've read about that,' he said. 'I think…' But he was interrupted by Richard Bentham.

'Definitely the graves of Jewish soldiers. A pile of stones

over the grave is supposed to help them rest in peace,' he stated. Ben smiled a thank you, and caught up with Paula, who seemed to be muttering quietly to herself as she hung on to her hat in the stiff breeze. He arrived alongside her just in time to catch 'To you, from failing hands we throw the torch' and stood silent beside her as she finished the poem.

'I didn't know that was on the syllabus,' he said, making light of what had, in truth, been a moving moment.

'It isn't,' she replied. 'I memorised it, as my little tribute to the fallen. I was determined to recite it here.' They were interrupted by the voice of the guide.

'Back to the coach if you please, ladies and gentlemen,' he said. 'Our next stop is the German cemetery of Langemark.'

Comparing notes over dinner that evening, opinion was divided over which was the most moving memorial, but united in comments on Langemark. 'Grim,' was how most summed it up.

'It's because the stones are dark,' said Paula. 'And flat on the ground. The information on them is terribly sad as it is at Tyne Cot and every other memorial I've ever visited. So many young men. So many men not identified, especially from the 1914–1918 war. But even so, there's something uplifting about the curving lines of white stones even if it's saddening. Those black squares lying flat to the ground at the Langemark cemetery – each marking where six or more bodies are buried – even without the hints on the information boards that the young volunteers were lied to about what they were to face; those are just one long cry of the futility of war.'

Ben nodded.

'And interestingly, everyone was affected in the same

way. The conversation at the table was all about the differences between the two traditions,' replied Ben.

'Except round our friend Gwyn,' remarked Paula. 'His conversation was all about the poor service at lunch and how his omelette was rubbery. You know he's planning to go ashore again this evening for "a civilised drink in the hotel by the river"?'

'So much for his bad hip then. I hope he's left his poor wife in peace.'

'You must be joking. I saw her hobbling off to the gangplank as we left the bar and came down here.'

'I hope you warned her about the wind. That big sunhat of hers isn't going to last five minutes even with her hat pin. It's definitely passed "blows the froth off your beer" and is headed for "blows your beer mug over."'

Blake laughed. 'A variant on the Beaufort scale?' he asked.

'That's right,' agreed Ben. 'Formulated for coarse sailors on the Norfolk Broads, who traditionally spend more time in the pub than on the water. That reminds me, Paula, where are we going tomorrow?'

'Ship sails at 11pm then it's on up river and another stop tomorrow morning. We've signed up for the visit to Arnhem and Oosterbeek.'

'OK. After that, I hope we get a free day or two. I could do with some lounging around time.'

'We can do that any day we want. Teflon Tess can't make us turn up on parade, you know.'

'So you say. We'll see. Tell you what though,' he said privately to Paula. 'Let's sit somewhere else at breakfast. There's a limit to how much I want to see of Gwyn, no matter how sorry I feel for Gwen.'

Chapter 3

Neither of the 2Gs, as some of the passengers had taken to calling them, were apparent at breakfast and everyone heaved a sigh of relief.

'There's always one on every cruise,' said Alec. 'One couple everyone avoids like the plague. On this one, there's two.'

'Oh,' said Ben curiously. 'Which is the other TBA?'

'TBA? Oh, got you,' said Alec. 'To Be Avoided. Haven't you met the Poison Pen?'

'No, I don't think we've had that pleasure,' said Paula. 'Which is he, or she?'

'He. It's the bloke with unrealistically red hair. Usually sits at the front of the bus, knows everything about everything and contradicts the guide. Someone christened him the Poison Pen because he's always leaving messages for Teflon Tess. Even her non-stick coating was showing some signs of wear last night.'

'Oh, you mean Richard. We met him at the airport,'

exclaimed Ben. Paula laughed and chipped in.

'He reminds me of George Eliot. You know. "Blessed is he who, having nothing to say, abstains from giving us ample evidence of the fact."

'Wow, that's cutting,' said Ben, a little surprised. 'But you're the cruise expert,' he said to Alec. 'Is it always like this?'

'Oh yes,' said the cruise veteran. 'There's always a vast majority of PPPs (perfectly pleasant people to you) and a couple of TBAs. It's what adds to the entertainment value. The people watching.'

By the close of the visit to Arnhem, Paula was bubbling with enthusiasm for the museum and Ben was sounding off about the, as he called it, 'functional illiteracy' of some of their fellow passengers.

'I mean,' he said, 'which bit of "one way only, if you enter here you must complete the route" wasn't clear?'

Paula sniggered. 'I thought you were going to have words with those two who tried to go back through the one-way doors,' she said. 'And as for the Poison Pen, I know you thought I was cruel earlier, but I thought you were going to pop one on him. What he didn't know about trench warfare clearly wasn't worth knowing.'

'It was when he started putting me straight about the secret auxiliary units in England I had to breathe hard,' admitted Ben. 'He knew absolutely sod all about it. Even when I said we'd visited one on land belonging to a friend, he kept rabbiting on.'

'And on. Did you hear his comments on the Arnhem museum? Apparently they got that wrong as well. He was making notes for Tess.'

'Poor old girl,' said Ben. 'And I didn't think I'd be saying that any time soon. Are you ready for a day off tomorrow?'

'Lead me to it,' said Paula with feeling. 'Tonight we've got the Dixie band, then it's bed for me and a day sunning myself on deck tomorrow.'

At dinner, a quick look over the shoulder to establish the whereabouts of the TBAs made it plain that the two Gs were missing again. Paula was sufficiently disturbed as to ask the maître d' if they were OK.

'I understand they're dining in their suite, madam,' he replied. 'It seems the gentleman is finding the crowd on board a little trying.' It was said without a trace of irony, no matter how hard Paula inspected his impassive visage.

'I see,' she said. 'So long as they're OK. Thank you.'

Early the following morning, Ben was leaning on their balcony rail admiring the slowly changing view, when he heard shouts from the deck above, then running feet and more shouts. He turned to the bed and snatched up shorts and a T-shirt.

'Where're you off?' asked a still sleepy Paula.

'On deck. I think the last shout was for a first aider. I'm going to see if they need any help.'

'It's only 5.30,' exclaimed Paula, but the door had already closed behind her husband.

She lay back on the pillows, contemplated returning to sleep, then sighed and like Ben pulled on some clothes. 'Might as well see what's up,' she muttered to herself.

It had taken Ben only a matter of moments to reach the companionway to the top deck and run up it. From that angle, all he could see was a small crowd of about four men between the stern and the ship's bridge. As he went forward one of the shapes came towards him and he saw it was not a crewman but Tess, looking shocked and green.

'Please return to your cabin,' she said. 'There's been an accident and this deck is now out of bounds to passengers.'

'I'm a first responder,' replied Ben, and as she looked confused, 'a sort of paramedic, and I've experience both as a nurse and in the police. I'll leave if you wish but I might be able to help.'

'Oh,' she hesitated, irresolute. 'OK. Come this way, then.'

She led Ben back towards the small huddle that parted as they approached.

'He's a paramedic,' she said to the captain. 'He might be able to help.'

'A first responder,' corrected Ben, but his words faded away as he saw on the ground before him a man with half his head caved in and wide blood spatter on the deck.

Chapter 4

'Please, everyone stand back,' commanded Ben, then he turned to the captain. 'I'm sorry, sir, the authority is yours, I know, but it's vital this scene is preserved as untouched as possible and it's clearly too late to do anything to help the casualty. Has this been reported to the local police?'

'Not yet,' said Tess, with a quick glance at the captain. 'Clearly we'll need to report it at our next port, but he's only just been found and we thought at first he might still be alive.'

Ben was kneeling by the body, his fingers on the carotid artery.

'No chance,' he said. 'And judging by how cool he feels, I suspect he's been dead for a while. Stop that,' he said suddenly. A young crewman had approached with a bucket and squeegee and seemed ready to wash down the stained wall and decking. 'Like I said, nothing must be touched until the police get here.'

The crewman looked at his captain and seemed inclined to continue with his task, so Ben took the bucket off him and put it safely out of the way.

'I suggest you set a guard on this area to keep everyone away, confine the passengers and as many crew as are not needed to sail the ship below this top deck, and report to the police ASAP.' Ben addressed his remarks impartially to Tess and the captain. This time it was the captain who responded.

'The man clearly ignored the guidance about low bridges,' he said. 'Or locks. We've come through several during the night. Is tragic accident. Thank you for your help, Mr…?'

'Asheton,' said Ben. 'Ben Asheton.'

'But we need not make too much fuss about this,' went on the captain. 'Tess will ring the police when we reach our next port.'

'I think she needs to ring them now,' said Ben stubbornly. 'You may be right, sir, but the rule is, until it is proved otherwise, you take all the precautions appropriate to a suspicious death. I do assure you, the police will appreciate a heads-up and will attend any sudden death by trauma, as this is.'

The captain produced a hollow laugh. 'Then perhaps you can tell me which police,' he said. 'The police in the Netherlands where we were yesterday? Or the police in Germany where we are now?'

Ben paused, floored for a moment, then said with confidence, 'Both. I would advise the German police of our ETA in Koblenz. And notify the Dutch police as well, as a courtesy. Then leave them to sort it out between them. By the way,' he added. 'Does anyone recognise the casualty?'

‘It’s Mr Richard Bentham,’ said Tess.

‘Richard Bentham?’ asked Ben, taking a closer look. ‘Are you sure? I didn’t recognise him without,’ he amended what he was going to say and finished, ‘without the red hair.’

‘I’m sure,’ said Tess. ‘His room key was in his shirt pocket and I recognise the suite number. He heads…he headed all his notes to me with it.’

‘Then someone should lock his suite as well and make sure no one disturbs it. I believe he was travelling alone?’

‘Yes, that’s right.’

Captain Maurice straightened up suddenly from the half crouch from which he had been examining the casualty. He removed his uniform hat, scratched his head through the thick thatch of black hair and put the hat back. For the first time, Ben saw the decision and command that must go with the role bearing responsibility for over 300 lives.

‘Stefan,’ he looked around for his second officer. ‘Take over the bridge until we moor in Koblenz, or until I give you a new destination. Paulo and Franz.’ He was looking at the two crew members in black polo shirts and trousers. ‘Mount a guard at the top of the companionway and make sure no one accesses this deck. I don’t want you to come any closer to the casualty than that. Tess, see everyone off this deck and lock all the doors as soon as we have left it. I will ring the police. OK. Everyone off.’ He waved his arms about as though shepherding them off the deck. Tess opened her mouth to protest, then at a look from the captain, closed it again. Ben and the captain were the last two to regain the reception area on the deck below.

‘You, Mr Asheton,’ said the captain, ‘you will come with me, if you please, to speak to the police. You seem to know

what you're talking about.' Heading down to the deck below, he turned suddenly on his heel. 'Tess,' he said, 'put the Deck 2 steward on guard outside Mr Bentham's cabin. He's not to move until I say so. I will make an announcement over the Tannoy when I have spoken to the police.' He set off again at a brisk walk and Ben followed, just as Paula appeared in reception, her mouth open to ask a question.

'Tell you later,' hissed Ben. 'I've got to go with the captain.' And he hurried after him, leaving Paula open-mouthed.

The captain's accommodation was larger than Ben's so-called suite, but not by much. One end was occupied by a bed, wardrobe and two easy chairs; the other by a desk with a chair either side. The captain took one and gestured to Ben to take the other. Then he picked up a mobile phone and dialled 110. When a call handler responded, clearly audible to Ben sitting opposite, the captain replied in what sounded like fluent German. After a pause and some further conversation, Captain Maurice held the phone out to Ben.

'Tell them what you saw and the conclusions you have reached,' he said.

Ben took the phone a shade nervously.

'I don't speak German,' he said. 'At least not beyond "Zwei bier bitte".'

'Don't worry, I told them that was so,' said the captain with a faint smile. 'You are British after all. Just tell them what you know.' Ben turned to the phone, ignoring the probably justifiable slur on British language abilities.

'I'm sorry, I don't speak German. I gather you can understand English,' he said.

'That is so,' said a precise, slightly accented male voice on the other end. 'I am Detective Muller of the Kriminalpolizei. Please describe to me what you found this morning.'

Ben paused for a moment, marshalling his thoughts.

'I went on to the top deck of the *River Diamond* at around 5.30 this morning. I saw a small group of people near the wheelhouse. As I went towards them I saw a casualty lying on the ground and I went forward to offer my help. I'm a first responder at home in England. That's a sort of paramedic.' He added, 'I've been one ever since I retired from the police.'

'Ah,' said Detective Muller. 'Ex police – good. Go on, please.'

'My initial assessment was that the casualty was dead and had probably been so for some hours. He had a major blunt force trauma to the back of his head, which had crushed his skull. Brain matter was apparent in the immediate surroundings as well as blood. It did not look like a survivable injury. I felt for his carotid pulse and there was none, and his skin was cold. I then stepped back and advised Captain Maurice that the body should not be disturbed further and the incident should be reported to you. The only part of the body I touched was his neck.'

'Thank you,' said Detective Muller. 'That is very clear. Who was present on the deck when you arrived?'

'Captain Maurice, the cruise director Tess (sorry I don't know her surname), and two, no, three crew members. I think that was all.'

'And why had you gone on deck at that early hour?' asked the detective.

'I was on the balcony of my cabin, enjoying the views, and I heard voices. They sounded panicky and one said something about first aid. I thought I should offer my help.'

'Thank you. Please pass me back to Captain Maurice.'

There was a further exchange in German, then Captain Maurice rang off and put the phone down with a sigh. He leaned back in his chair and said, 'Coffee? It has already been a bad day, and it's hardly started.' Turning to the coffee maker behind him, he went on, 'They wanted to know how you could hear what was said on deck. I was explaining the layout of the boat and that, if your cabin was on the side where we were standing, you would likely be able to hear very clearly what was going on.'

He turned back with two mugs full of dark coffee. 'Lucky for me you woke up early, and lucky also that it was so early no one else did. Or we'd have been flooded by tourists taking photos. Milk?'

'No thanks.' Ben took the coffee. 'I'm sorry if I was disrespectful up there,' he said. 'I didn't mean to be. I was just concerned the police should know we did everything right.'

'No, you were right,' said the captain. 'I was letting Tess and her worries about the tour management override my good sense. You spoke up at the right moment. And if the managers don't like it they can…' He paused, searching for the right phrase.

'Take a running jump?' suggested Ben.

'That will do,' said the captain, with the first smile Ben had seen.

There was a further pause for coffee drinking before Ben said, 'Forgive me for asking, but I get the impression you're not too keen on mixing with the passengers?'

'Not too keen?' queried the captain.

'Not happy.'

'Ah. Yes. No, not too keen on the large groups. In small

groups, yes, but I did not train as a seaman to make speeches. And all the…' He waved a expressive hand.

'All the Tess-ness?' suggested Ben.

'Yes, all the Tess-ness is a bit too much. She does a good job,' he added in a hurry. 'But it is not *my* job.'

'So I guess you don't know much about the victim, Richard Bentham.'

'Probably less than you,' replied the captain. 'I know from the passenger list he was travelling solo; and judging by the fact he booked a double not a single cabin, he didn't need to budget. Apart from that, all I know is he had a lot of opinions he was eager to share.'

Ben finished his coffee. 'I should be getting back to my wife,' he said. 'She'll be getting worried. And I need to get dressed properly before the police come on board.'

'Yes, they will want to speak to you. Thank you, Mr Asheton.'

'Ben,' said Ben, holding out his hand.

'Luc,' said the captain. And shook it.

Back in their cabin, Ben's main preoccupation was a super-swift shower and shave before seeing the German police. Over the sound of rushing water and razor he did his best to answer Paula's increasingly impatient questions. When he came out of the bathroom he found her putting clean chinos and a white shirt out on the bed.

'You'd better look professional,' she said. 'You don't want them treating you as a suspect.'

'I think I already am, judging by the questions about why did I go on deck. But that's only to be expected. OK. I'm going to go up to reception and let the captain know I'm available when needed.'

'I'll be up in a minute,' said Paula. 'Get some breakfast while you can. I won't be far behind.'

As soon as Ben left the cabin she seized her phone, checked her contacts and placed a call.

'Geldard,' said a familiar voice.

'Greg,' said Paula with relief. 'You're not going to believe this, but we've got a suspicious body on board.'

The reception area was filled with passengers milling around in gossipy circles when Ben arrived. He was instantly pounced on by Blake and Pen.

'What d'you know?' demanded Blake without preamble. 'We've been told only that there's been an incident and no one's allowed on deck, but there's a rumour flying that you've been involved.'

'Rumour? From where?' asked Ben, trying to prevaricate.

'Pen had it from our deck steward, who had it from someone in the crew. So come on. Spill them.'

'Not much to say,' replied Ben. 'Just that there's been a fatality and, as with any sudden death, the police have been informed. I assume they'll be coming on board when we moor at Koblenz.'

'An accident?' asked Pen.

'That's for the police to decide,' said Ben. 'Now, I need to get some breakfast while I can, because I think the police will want to talk to me, since it was me who pronounced them dead.'

'Who was it?' asked Blake. 'Anyone we know?'

'I really don't think I should say anymore,' said Ben. 'I believe the captain will be making an announcement.'

Even as he spoke, the Tannoy gave a crackle, and Tess's voice announced, 'Please, everyone, stand by for an important message from the captain.'

There was another crackle, then Captain Maurice's voice said, 'I am sorry to tell you that one of our passengers suffered an accident in the night and we expect both police and an ambulance to meet us when we dock in Koblenz. Would everyone please take their breakfast as usual, then return to their cabins until called into the main lounge. It is unlikely that the tours planned for today will go ahead as scheduled but we will advise you further as soon as we know more. We will certainly get your cruise back to normal as soon as we can. In the meantime, my apologies for the inconvenience.' There was a click as the Tannoy fell silent.

'Well, that'll give the Poison Pen something to complain about,' remarked Blake. Ben said nothing, as he headed for the stairs and his breakfast.

Chapter 5

Ben had just stabbed the top of his eggs Benedict, releasing a golden flood of yolk right across the white plate, when there was a disturbance by the restaurant door. He was stirring the yolk into the hollandaise, thoughtfully making tie-dye patterns in the sauce, when he became aware of Tess moving to intercept the lady waving her arms about in the doorway. Paula, with the better view, remarked, 'Something seems to have upset Gwen.'

The first delicious forkful in his mouth, Ben mumbled something inaudible, swallowed hard then said again, 'Can you hear what she's saying?' As he spoke he turned, then said, 'Oh oh. That's not just another complaint about bitter coffee.' Paula too was rising to her feet, leaving her crispy bacon and scrambled egg to cool. They both dropped their cutlery and moved towards the door, wiping mouths on napkins.

By this time Tess had edged Gwen into the anteroom

beside the restaurant entrance, by the simple expedient of moving forward so that the other woman, perforce, had to move backward. She had her hand on Gwen's arm, and when Paula reached them was saying, 'Come to my office, Gwen, and let's sort this out quietly.' Paula brushed past and put her arm round the older woman, whose face was streaked with tears mixing with the long hair straggling down to her shoulders.

'What's the problem, Gwen?' she asked gently. 'Can we help?'

Instantly Gwen turned to Paula and buried her head in her shoulder. Standing behind, all Ben could hear was, 'It's Gwyn. He's missing and everyone's saying he must be the dead body on deck. But she won't let me see him.' She pointed a shaking finger at Tess and then howled into Paula's shoulder again.

Between them, Paula and Ben lowered Gwen into the chair behind her and Ben knelt in front of her, taking her hands in his.

'Look at me, Gwen,' he said in a quiet but commanding tone. 'Look at me.' When he was sure he'd got her attention he went on. 'The casualty on deck is *not* Gwyn. Do you hear me? It's not Gwyn. I promise you that.' Gwen gulped and shuddered, clutching at Ben's hands. 'Do you understand me?' said Ben. 'It's not Gwyn. Now, take a deep breath. And another. No, don't say anything yet. Just take another deep breath. There's plenty of time.

'Get her a drink of water,' he said over his shoulder to Tess, and nodded to Paula to pull a chair up and sit down close to Gwen. The water appeared and he handed it to Paula.

'Let her take sips of that,' he said, then turned his

attention to Gwen again. 'OK, now tell me what's happened. When did you last see Gwyn?'

'When we went to bed,' said Gwen. 'My knees were playing up after all the walking yesterday, so I took a sleeping pill when I went to bed. That's the last I remember until this morning, when I woke up and Gwyn wasn't there. He never gets up without a cup of tea first. Well, he might get up to go to the bathroom, you know, but not get up properly without his cup of tea. I make it for him every morning first thing. But he wasn't in bed and he wasn't in the bathroom. And when I came to look for him they wouldn't let me go on deck and they wouldn't let me go into the lounge and then everyone was talking about a dead body on deck and the police and an ambulance and I just knew it was Gwyn.' The voice, which was rising again, suddenly cut off. 'But you say it isn't Gwyn. Is it true? It isn't Gwyn? You're sure there's no mistake? Because if it isn't Gwyn, who is it? And where's Gwyn?'

The last words were almost a shout and then she broke down in torrents of tears.

Ben looked up into the horror-struck face of Tess. 'That's the question, isn't it?' he said. 'You'll tell the captain?'

'Yes.' She took a deep breath and visibly pulled herself together. 'First thing, we need to organise a search of the ship. After that…' She paused. 'Well, first things first. I'll sort that. Can you take Gwen into the lounge? I'll tell the staff to settle you in a quiet corner and to bring you coffee, toast, whatever you'd like. I'll report back ASAP.'

'OK,' said Ben. 'Come on, Gwen, come to the lounge while the staff search the ship.'

'No. I must go with them,' exclaimed Gwen.

'Go where?' asked Paula practically. 'No, Gwen, let all

the fit young men and women search the ship. They'll be much quicker if you and I aren't in their way.'

Between them, Ben and Paula got Gwen to her feet and moving in the direction of the lift to the deck above and the lounge. Tess nodded her gratitude and whisked off in the direction of the captain's cabin. Behind her, Ben was aware of many pairs of eyes, staring curiously from the restaurant.

Scarcely an hour had passed when the captain joined Ben, Paula and Gwen at the little group of chairs in the corner, Tess tagging along behind. Ben caught his eye as they approached, and he shook his head slightly before sitting down.

'I'm sorry, Mrs Rees, but I'm afraid after a thorough search of the ship, we have failed to find your husband.' He was going to go on, but Gwen interrupted him.

'No,' she said. 'You can't have searched it all yet. It's a big ship. How many cabins? Seventy? And that's just for passengers. You need to do a proper search. Try again. Go on.' And she waved him away.

The captain didn't move. 'It was a *very* thorough search,' he said. 'We used every member of crew, hotel and office staff not directly involved in sailing the ship or serving breakfast. That was a total of twenty-eight people spread over the three decks. We even searched the engine spaces. I'm sorry, Mrs Rees, but Mr Rees is definitely not on board.'

'Then where is he?' asked Gwen blankly. 'We came back on board together last night. Where else can he be?'

Captain Maurice looked at Tess with an interrogative eyebrow.

'I've checked the database,' she said. 'Mr and Mrs Rees checked in on board with their barcodes at 2106 and 2108 hours respectively. They didn't check out again. They were on board when we sailed.'

'If Mr Rees was on board when we sailed, as it seems he was,' said the captain, 'then the only remaining explanation is that he somehow fell overboard during the night. We made no stops where he could have stepped ashore.' He stood up. 'I'm very sorry, Mrs Rees,' he said, 'but I must report this also to the police. They will want to know what your husband was wearing and whether he had any identification on him.'

'But I don't know,' wailed Gwen. 'I was asleep. I told you, I took a sleeping pill.'

'How about we go to your cabin and see what's missing?' suggested Paula. 'Tess and I can come with you.' The captain nodded his consent and between them the two women shepherded the weeping third out of the lounge and down to the Rees's cabin.

Ben got to his feet and followed as the captain left the lounge. 'Luc,' he said quietly, 'are you thinking this disappearance may be linked to the casualty on deck?'

Luc Maurice paused. 'Two incidents like this on the same night. It seems not likely they are,' he hesitated, 'coincidence?'

Ben nodded. 'I think you're right,' he said. 'They *could* be unconnected but that would be very strange. If I can make another suggestion? It might be wise to keep Mrs Rees away from the other passengers until the police have spoken to her. And have a seal put on their cabin too, once she's had a look through it with Paula and Tess. Is there another cabin she could be accommodated in?'

'Yes, I will speak with Tess when she comes back. We can do that.'

‘What’re the chances of finding the body in the river?’ Ben asked as an afterthought.

‘Better than 50:50 I would think,’ replied Luc. ‘Our route last night was through a fairly busy part of the river. If a body washed up somewhere, there’s a good chance it would be found. Identifying it, well…’ And he shrugged.

Chapter 6

Left alone, Ben hesitated, then turned back to the lounge.

'Waste not, want not,' he muttered, and with sad recollections of his uneaten eggs Benedict he picked up a piece of toast and smothered it in butter and marmalade. This time, the interruption was his phone buzzing in his pocket. 'Greg,' he said in surprise through a mouthful of toast. 'Why do I have the pleasure…oh I get it.' He interrupted himself. 'Don't tell me. Paula's been on to you.'

'Of course,' said Greg. 'Well, clearly the good news is you haven't been arrested yet.'

'We haven't docked yet!' replied Ben. 'But it seems there might be another body.'

'You have all the luck,' replied Greg. 'Seriously though, if you need a word in an ear, let me know. I don't know whether I can do anything, but I can at least vouch for your good character. So, what's with the second body. Male? Female?

Old or young? Come on, don't hold out on a friend.'

'At the moment it's just a missing person, but it seems likely he went into the river as he disappeared while we were sailing last night. They've already searched the ship and he's definitely not on board.'

'Connected to the other death Paula told me about?'

'Don't know, but seems unlikely to be a coincidence.' Ben described the circumstances around the death of the red-headed Richard Bentham. 'What puzzles me, though, is how two people could separately be stupid enough to be hit by a bridge. And if it wasn't an idiotic accident, what on earth could connect Mr Richard Bentham and Mr Gwyn Rees? They showed no signs of having met before when we were all hanging about at the airport.'

'Always investigate the victim,' recommended Greg. 'That's the best starting point; but of course it's not really your business. I should be saying, leave it to the German police!'

'Provided they don't suspect me,' said Ben, but he stopped as he realised the ship's engines had changed note. He looked out of the window. 'We're coming into dock,' he said. 'I think I need to go, Greg. The German police will want to talk to me.'

'OK, I won't keep you,' said Greg. 'But do keep me posted, and I'll give the locals a ring if it'll help.'

Two plain-clothed police and two uniforms came aboard the moment the gangplank was down, accompanied by what Ben guessed to be mortuary staff. On the bank he could see a plain van and a couple of liveried police cars drawn up in a row. He stayed in the lounge as the police were greeted by Captain Maurice and Tess. He was so engrossed with watching what was going on, Paula was sitting down next to him before he realised she'd returned.

'Any news?' he asked.

'Well, it's a bit odd,' said Paula. 'Tess and I went down to their cabin with Gwen and helped her go through their stuff. She reckons there's a pair of trousers and a shirt missing and a pair of deck shoes. But she's no idea why he would've gone back on deck. It was while we were sorting that out that Tess noticed the towelling robes were missing too. My immediate thought was it might have made sense if one was missing, because he might have been struggling to sleep and wandered up on deck in his dressing gown. But he wouldn't have been wearing two, so where was the other one? Then Gwen said they'd never had any towelling robes, and Tess went off on one because all cabins are supposed to have robes and slippers. When I came up she was giving some poor cabin maid hell for not doing her job properly.' Paula fell silent as Captain Maurice returned with a couple of German police in tow. The first held out his hand to Ben.

'We spoke earlier,' he said. 'I am Detective Muller. Is this your wife?' He turned to Paula.

'Yes,' said Ben, performing the introductions. 'How can I help?'

Detective Muller was a stocky man with light brown hair and eyes of indeterminate colour. 'In fact,' as Ben said after to Paula, 'you'd be hard put to describe him to anyone.' He was generally colourless in every way, almost every feature just plain average, adding up to an appearance that would be easy to hide in a crowd. His clothes completed the effect, light-blue, short-sleeved shirt over dark trousers, and the sort of loose jacket that almost everyone wears but no one is very excited about. It didn't entirely escape Ben's notice that the looseness of the jacket was not just a lack of fashion statement but cover for a firearm. He sat down in one of the chairs round the coffee table and took out a recorder.

'I think I have the basics from Captain Maurice,' he said, 'but can you tell me your version, how you came to be involved? You are OK with a recording?' and he waved the small device before putting it between them on the table. Ben embarked on his story, unsurprised that Detective Muller was particularly interested in why he'd gone on deck, and asked a lot of questions about what had disturbed him.

Finally Muller leant back in his chair and turned the recorder off.

'It seems I am to thank you for keeping the crime scene…' He hesitated. 'Clean? Undisturbed? What you have said confirms what the captain said. I thank you.'

'What happens now?' asked Ben.

'The body is off for an autopsy. We will then see what we find.'

'You don't buy the collision-with-a-bridge theory?'

There was a pause while Detective Muller worked out what the colloquialism meant, then he said, 'Shall I say, there is some question.' Ben glanced round to see who else was in earshot, and noting that they had been accorded privacy for the interrogation by the police, he said, 'The blood spatter?'

He got a sharp glance from Muller.

'You noticed that?'

'I just managed to prevent a deckhand from washing it off, and that meant I got a close look. It didn't seem to match the explanation.'

'So I think too. But I should not say more.' He paused.

'One other thing. What do you know about the casualty, Mr Richard Bentham?'

'Not much,' replied Ben. 'Just that he wore a red toupee that wasn't very convincing and was travelling on his own. And that he had a lot of confidence in his own knowledge. I believe he made a lot of complaints to the cruise director, Tess. Not much else.'

'OK. I think that will do for now. You may go.'

'Thank you.' Ben stood up and shook the extended hand again. 'Are you dealing with the missing person as well?'

'I am in contact with my Dutch colleagues,' he replied, with another sharp look. 'If they find anything they will let me know. You think they are connected?'

'Big coincidence if not.'

'As you say. OK. We may speak again, Mr Asheton.'

'Ben,' said Ben.

'Carl,' said the policeman, for the first time with a smile.

Chapter 7

Ben returned to Paula, but whatever she was going to say was overridden by a Tannoy announcement from Tess.

'Good morning,' she said. 'I'm sorry to tell you that two of the tours arranged for today have had to be cancelled. However, I'm hopeful the local walking tour can go ahead after lunch and we may also be able to run the bike trip, with a shortened route. In the meantime, we would be delighted to welcome you to the lounge for a quiz, and lunch will be at the slightly earlier time of 12.30. So, let's all give it up for keeping on keeping on!'

A very thin scatter of applause was just audible around the ship.

'Quiz?' asked Paula with a raised eyebrow.

'No thanks,' said Ben. 'Let's go down to our cabin. I want a word in private.'

*

As they went down the Deck 2 companionway Ben noted that crime tape was still across two cabin doors just four doors down from theirs on the port side. He paused at their door.

'I hadn't realised the Rees's and Bentham were in adjacent cabins!'

'No. Nor had I,' said Paula, opening their door. 'But then, no reason why I would. I've no idea who's where, unless I've seen them coming or going.' They went into the cabin and Paula made to open the sliding door onto their balcony.

'No, not out there,' said Ben. 'We'll be overheard and I want a private talk.'

He sat down on the bed and leaned on the headboard. Paula sat in a chair by the dressing table and looked at him.

'What's the problem?' she asked. 'I know you. Something's bothering you.'

'When you were with Gwen, did she happen to say anything about Bentham?' asked Ben.

'I don't think so,' said Paula. 'It was all about Gwyn and how long they'd been together and what a wonderful man he was and how much she missed him.'

'OK, so, when she was talking about Gwyn, did she happen to mention if he could swim?'

'No, I don't think that came up. Why? Where are you going with this, Ben?'

Ben picked at the duvet cover for a moment, then said, 'This goes no further than us, Paula. The police asked me to keep quiet. But the blood spatter on deck, it didn't fit with the explanation of an accident with a bridge.'

'Why? And what's that got to do with Gwyn? What…'

'Hang on, Paula. Let's have one question at a time. Captain Maurice put forward the theory that Bentham had come on deck when he shouldn't have, and been hit on the head by a low bridge while the ship was sailing last night. But I saw the blood spatter. In fact, I just managed to stop a deckhand washing it off the deck. And that's the point. I can't see how any bridge could hit a head at the right angle for the blood to land where it did on the deck, even if the wheelhouse forrard was retracted into its housing because a bridge was approaching. The blood would land in a spray down the deck, in line with the forward movement of the ship. While what we actually had was the spatter you'd expect to see if someone had been hit by a good old blunt implement swung from port to starboard.'

'OK. Makes sense. Do the police agree with you?'

'Yes, I think so.'

'So what's this got to do with Gwyn?'

'On the basis that a missing person and a dead body on the same night are an unlikely coincidence, then either Gwyn is prime suspect for the murder, or there was a fight during which he managed to land a lethal blow before he was injured and went over the side.'

'Oh boy!' Paula was silent for a moment. 'And which do you think it is?'

'I don't have much evidence either way at the moment, but in terms of probability, the first seems more likely than the second. I guess it all depends on what they find when or if they find Gwyn's body.'

'No body equals he's the murderer?'

'Not necessarily. To paraphrase Greg, no evidence of a body doesn't necessarily mean no body.'

They were interrupted by yet another cough from the Tannoy.

‘I thought she said she didn’t like using that thing,’ said Ben irritably.

‘I suppose strange times mean different approaches,’ said Paula. ‘Come on. That’s lunch. And we missed most of breakfast.’

No sooner had they sat down with Pen and Blake, when Tess came bustling up with Gwen in tow.

‘Would you mind looking after Gwen?’ she said, nodding significant looks in their direction, which she clearly fondly imagined to be invisible to Gwen. ‘You know.’ And she nodded again.

Paula pulled out the chair next to her.

‘Sit here, Gwen,’ she suggested. ‘I think you’re very sensible and very brave to try to keep going.’ Blake leaned over and poured her a glass of water from the jug on the table.

‘And I’m sure we all hope for good news soon,’ he said with false heartiness. The conversation languished at that point, but luckily the steward appeared with the menus and everyone looked down at the choices before them with relief.

Order placed, Blake asked, ‘Was it you I saw talking to the police, Ben? Did they say how long we’ll be held up here?’

‘Yes, and no,’ replied Ben. ‘I understand Mr Bentham’s body has been taken for an autopsy, and the police are pursuing their enquiries. When they’ve finished with us I’m sure we’ll be told.’ He turned to Gwen. ‘I hadn’t realised you had adjacent cabins,’ he said. ‘Did you see much of your neighbour?’ Ben jerked as Paula landed a vicious kick under the table and he shuffled in his seat to move his legs out of the way.

'Not much,' said Gwen, between mouthfuls of mushroom omelette, which she'd pronounced, 'Easy to eat, see.'

'Oh, I wondered if you and Gwyn had chatted with him.'

'Ow,' exclaimed Blake, reaching down to rub his ankle.

'Sorry,' said Paula, glaring at Ben. 'Mistaken identity.'

'Not a very nice man,' stated Gwen suddenly. 'Always bossing people about. Always right, if you know what I mean. I can't be doing with bossy myself.' Her listeners, remembering the way Gwyn had sent her hither and yon on errands, were rendered silent by this pronouncement and the conversation went into terminal decline.

At the end of the meal Ben, limping only slightly, caught up with Gwen outside the lounge. 'I'm glad you were able to join us for lunch,' he said. 'You missed everything yesterday.'

'That's right,' she said. 'Gwyn likes his peace and quiet, so we ate in our room yesterday.'

The afternoon passed quietly enough. Around half of the passengers went off on the two remaining tours; the rest enjoyed the sun on their balconys or took a siesta in their cabins. Ben and Paula were among the sun lovers, and while Paula read her Kindle, Ben stared into space, his mind busy behind his sunglasses. At least, until sleep overtook him.

Just before dinner, they went down to their cabin to shower the sun lotion off and change. They were surprised to find a flashing light on their phone and a message asking Ben to join the captain in the wheelhouse. Ben looked at his watch.

'I'll whip up and see him now,' he said, 'then come back to change. OK?'

Paula nodded, already halfway into the shower.

'Of course. See you in a minute.'

Arriving at the wheelhouse, Ben hovered by the door, not entirely sure of the etiquette for entry, but was spotted quickly by Luc Maurice, who beckoned him in.

'Come in, Ben,' he said. 'And thank you. Come on down to my quarters. I can leave this to my number two for now.'

In silence they went down the inner stair to the deck below and then on down to the crew quarters. Arriving in his cabin, Luc said, 'I am told the police are coming here again with an update, and hopefully to release us so that we can complete our cruise. I asked you to join us because I think you know something of their thoughts.'

'Oh,' said Ben, on his guard and not sure what else to say.

'I don't have your background and experience, Ben, but I am not a stupid man. I think you were suspicious of the circumstances of this death. And I think the police are too. I want them to share with me their thoughts, and I think you might help.'

Ben thought for a moment. 'If I can help I will,' he said. 'But I won't say or do anything that might prejudice their investigation. That would go against all my early training.'

'So you think there will be an investigation?'

'I don't know, but I think it likely. Why don't we wait and see what they say?'

Luc nodded, and busied himself with making coffee. 'I think perhaps a stronger drink might not be suitable,' he said. By the time the coffee was made there was a knock on the door and Carl Muller was waiting outside with a policewoman they hadn't seen before. All four in the small cabin was distinctly crowded, but Muller made no apology for the extra person.

'This is Officer Schneider,' he said. 'OK. The news is not good. We have the pathologist's findings. In short, they don't think the injury to Mr Bentham's head was due to collision with a bridge.' He paused, flicking over his notebook, and Ben said, 'May we ask why?'

'Many things,' said Muller. 'But mainly, there was no sign of grit or gravel in the wound, such as you would expect after collision with the concrete of a bridge. The wound was in fact perfectly clean. They also were of the view that the wound was the wrong shape, suggesting an ovoid, blunt instrument rather than a sharp edge. Moreover, our forensic team have checked both the deck and the two bridges the *Diamond* sailed under last night. There are no signs of a collision on either of the bridges, and the signs on the deck were not consistent with an accident. They were consistent with a deliberate blow to the head. So, Captain Maurice, this is now a murder enquiry.'

There was a silence, of the kind – as Ben reported later to Paula – best described as 'pregnant'.

'What does that mean for my ship and passengers?' asked the captain.

'For the ship, it means you must stay here in Koblenz until we are satisfied our enquiries are complete. For the passengers and crew, we will now undertake interviews of everyone on board. No one may leave until they have been questioned. No one may leave Germany until I say so, but after the interviews I would expect many of the passengers would be able to go on tours by coach until I can release the whole ship. That is the best I can do, Captain Maurice, and

I do appreciate you are in a difficult position.'

There was another pause, and Ben asked, 'Has the other passenger, Gwyn Rees, been found?'

'That is why Officer Schneider is here. I must go now and talk to Mrs Rees. We have scoured the river and its banks in the areas passed through by this ship last night, and some distance downstream of those areas as well. We have found nothing. So, we must conclude either that her husband is alive and is a suspect in a murder case, or that he is dead and we just haven't found his body yet. Either way.' He shrugged. 'It is bad news, I think.'

As Ben reported to Greg later, the passenger reactions were wholly predictable. The complainers complained, a lot. The drama queens of both genders went around in panicky groups, voicing oft-repeated concerns about being confined on a ship with a suspected murderer. The words 'like an Agatha Christie' were frequently heard. The snobs and proto racists assumed the perpetrator was a member of the crew and the remainder were excited to take the opportunity to observe a police investigation, up front and personal. Blake and Pen fell into the last group, which at least made them more cheerful to be around than most of the rest. The main problem for Ben was avoiding being trapped into giving away how much he knew, or guessed, about the police thinking.

The outlier to all of this was Gwen, who persisted, in the face of all evidence to the contrary, in promulgating the 'hit by a bridge' theory to explain both the demise of Mr Bentham and the disappearance of her husband – the latter fast becoming canonised in her remembrance. The discussion with Muller and Officer Schneider did not go smoothly.

She flatly refused to accept their interpretation of the facts, insisting that her husband would never have just left and must be in the river somewhere. Then she became hysterical, and finding Tess's ministrations unhelpful, Muller had called on Ben and Paula for assistance. Once she calmed down a little, Paula helped her along the corridor to the spare cabin allotted for her use while the police completed the search of hers. Tess had not helped by referring to it as 'a crime scene'!

Returning to Ben in their cabin, Paula was rather quiet.

'What's the matter?' demanded Ben, recognising the signs.

'Something's not right,' said Paula. 'Something doesn't ring true about how she's reacting.'

'Gwen, you mean?'

'Yes, of course I mean Gwen. What did you think about that hysteria?'

'You mean that emotional outburst? Well, it wasn't an anxiety attack for a start. None of the symptoms were right.'

'I think that's where I'm coming from,' said Paula. 'It felt like hysteria in the film sense, from someone who'd only seen it in an old Hollywood movie. She's not a happy bunny about being excluded from her cabin either.'

'I can imagine that is irritating,' said Ben, trying to be fair, 'but…'

'And another thing,' said Paula. 'Have you ever known a man come on holiday with five pairs of shoes?'

Ben thought about his flip flops, trainers and one pair of decent shoes for evening and grinned.

'You're asking me?' he said.

'Well, I saw the police going through their wardrobe

while I was with Gwen. There were four pairs of men's shoes in there. One pair of trainers, one pair of sandals, and two pairs of leather shoes, one black and one brown. The only things obviously missing were the slippers provided by the ship.'

'The slippers that Gwen says they didn't get, like they didn't get the towelling robes?'

'That's right.'

Ben got up and headed for the door.

'Where're you going?'

'To talk to the cabin maid. If I can find her.'

Chapter 8

By teatime the police had finished all the interviews with the passengers and were on the home straight as regarded the crew. Ben had caught the Deck 2 cabin maid as she came out of the conversation with the police and it was plain her feathers were ruffled.

'It not fair,' she said vehemently to anyone who would listen, which definitely included Ben. 'I do my job well. Tess have no right to shout at me. I put bathrobes in all the cabins. All.'

'And slippers?' asked Ben.

'Yes. And slippers. Who say I not put slippers out?' She stared round pugnaciously. 'No one,' said Ben hurriedly. 'I was just checking.'

'And if that cabin not clean, it not my fault. To clean I have to go in and for two, no, three days they not let me in. It not fair.' She turned to bustle off, and Ben followed her.

'What d'you mean?' he asked. 'Which days didn't you go in Gwen's cabin?'

She turned, breathless with indignation. 'Today, obviously. But also yesterday and the day before. They say they don't want to be disturbed. They hang the sign outside for two whole days. When I knock they say to go away. They eating in their cabin. And stewards deliver meals to their cabin.'

'Who told you to go away?'

'You not listening?' she demanded, then recollecting herself said, 'Sorry, sir. I mean they tell me to go away.'

'Both of them?' asked Ben.

'No. It was the lady. Mrs Rees.'

As she went away down the corridor, Ben stood irresolute, then making his mind up, he knocked on the door of the small bar where Muller was conducting his interviews.

'Come,' said a voice, and Ben went in, finding only Carl Muller and Officer Schneider.

'I don't know whether this is important,' said Ben, 'but I thought you should know if you didn't already. I don't think anyone other than Mrs Rees has seen Mr Rees since supper two days ago.'

'And you know this because?'

'The maid says she wasn't allowed in their cabin for those two days and I can tell you they had meals delivered to their cabin that day. I last saw him at supper the night before.'

'Which means?'

'If you're looking for a body you may need to look further downstream than you have so far. One other thing. It may be that he was wearing a towelling robe rather than trousers and shirt. At least, it seems two are missing.'

'The maid again?'

'Yes. The maid again.'

'You believe her?'

'Yes, I do.'

'Eva, get her back here now.' Officer Schneider nodded and went to the door. 'And thank you, Ben,' said Muller, reaching for the phone. 'It seems I need another word with my colleagues in the Netherlands. In the meantime, I think a chat with Mrs Rees at our office in town might be indicated.'

Chapter 9

Ben joined Paula in the lounge just as Mrs Rees was escorted off the ship by Officer Schneider. They made an odd pair going up the jetty side by side. One tall and slim, with blonde hair in a pony tail, smart uniform dark trousers and jacket. The other short and dumpy, grey hair in a bun tousled by the wind, still in crumpled pink cotton trousers and blue blouse, topped by the ubiquitous sun hat, apparently firmly skewered to the bun.

He sat down in the quiet corner and noted, with inward amusement, that a wide space was being left around them. 'It seems I'm contaminated by association.' Paula looked round and laughed briefly.

'I think we're being seen as spies in the camp,' she said. 'On the other hand, it gives me the chance to ask what you're thinking. What did you say to Muller?'

'That the only person who claims to have seen Rees the

day before yesterday is Gwen. Therefore we have only her word for it that he was on the ship at all. And if there is no sign of a body having gone overboard the night before last, then they should look further downstream.'

'And if they find him further downstream?'

'Then we need to ask ourselves, and her, why she pretended he was on board when he wasn't. Particularly if they find the body wearing a towelling robe. Or nothing.'

Paula pulled a face. 'Doesn't bear thinking about,' she said, without clarifying whether it was just the body or the nude body she found so distasteful. 'But I'm confused. Where does this leave Gwen? And what happened to Bentham?'

'Now, there's the problem. I have almost more theories than I have fingers. One, Gwyn was on board but hiding for some reason we don't yet know. He killed Bentham and then either fell overboard and hasn't been found yet, which seems unlikely, or he left the ship somehow and is on the run. Either way, Gwen must have a pretty good idea what happened and is covering up for him.

'Two, Gwyn went overboard twenty-four hours earlier than we thought and Gwen has been hiding his absence. If that was so, then he can't have had anything to do with Bentham's death. In that case, did Bentham kill Gwyn in collusion with Gwen? And did she fall out with him later and hit him over the head with something? Or did Gwen kill Gwyn and someone else killed Bentham in a bizarre coincidence?'

'Or did Gwen kill them both?' added Paula. 'Either way, I'm struggling for motive. I find it hard to imagine Gwen as the femme fatale, snaring Bentham into a plot to kill her egregious husband. And why would she kill Bentham after killing her husband?'

'And what about means?' added Ben. 'Opportunity, yes, I can see that. But motive and means – they're a problem. The difficulty is, we know so little about Richard Bentham. You know Greg always says, start with the victim.'

'Ah, I can help a bit there,' replied Paula. 'I've been talking to Tess. She said she wasn't surprised he behaved the way he did. That she'd seen it before in similar guests.'

'And what did she mean by that?'

'That's what I asked her. She said "bereaved".'

'Bereaved?'

'Yes. She said he'd lost his wife recently, and that she'd seen all that talking on and on before in someone recently bereaved. She said she put it down to loneliness. And that was why she wasn't very bothered by all his complaints She felt sorry for him.'

Ben was reduced to silence. Eventually he said, 'I feel ashamed. That I didn't notice. That I had less sensitivity than Tess.'

'Yes. I know what you mean. I feel the same. I suppose the truth is, she sees a lot of passengers. And she sees more than we gave her credit for.'

Chapter 10

That afternoon the German forensic team withdrew from the upper deck and indicated it could now be cleaned and made available to the passengers still trapped on board. It wasn't much of a compensation for the loss of their onward cruise, but the sun shone and some semblance of holiday mood reappeared as the majority took to the sun loungers and enjoyed topping up their tans. Ben and Paula managed to snag two of the couches right forward of the wheelhouse and would have enjoyed the relaxation but for a persistent worry that they were missing something.

'It really is none of our business,' said Paula for the umpteenth time.

'No, it's not, but I can't settle,' said Ben. 'I'm sure there's something I should have asked that maid and didn't.'

'You asked her about seeing Gwyn and about the clothes,' said Paula, her eyes in her book.

'I didn't ask her about the food,' exclaimed Ben, and Paula found she was addressing the empty air again.

Down one deck and Ben was hesitating before invading crew quarters, when Luc Maurice appeared on the stairs.

'I've had an idea,' he said. 'One that might help, perhaps.' He explained what he wanted and, 'Come with me,' said Luc.

The little cabin maid shared quarters with two others and was clearly thrown by finding the captain standing on the threshold.

'I wanted to ask you something,' explained Ben, and as she glanced back into the room behind her and at the two dark-haired girls sharing the small space, he said, 'It's fine. It won't take a moment. I wanted to ask what food was taken down to the Rees's cabin that day you didn't see Mr Rees.'

She looked puzzled. 'What you expect,' she replied. 'Breakfast. Two full English. Lunch. Soup and sandwiches. And cake. They didn't like anything they called foreign. And that evening, steak and chips and fruit salad.'

'Always two meals?'

'Yes. Always two.'

'Don't forget the drink,' chipped in one of the girls behind her. 'A whole bottle of champagne they had.' Ben, who was turning away, turned back sharply.

'Did they drink it all?' he asked.

'Don't know. Never saw it again.'

'You mean, you didn't clear the empty bottle away?'

'That's right. Either they drank it and lobbed the empty over the side. Very bad,' she said reprovingly. 'Or they didn't drink it and it's still in the cabin somewhere.'

'Thank you,' said Ben, looking at the captain. 'Can we go to your cabin, sir?'

'Of course.' He led the way.

'Why is that significant?' asked Luc Maurice.

'It may not be,' said Ben cautiously. 'But it does clear up one point. If Gwen was ordering two meals and her husband wasn't on board, then she was deliberately covering his absence. But the champagne. That's very interesting.'

'Why?'

'Because it would make a good blunt instrument. And if the bottle's not in the cabin, where is it?'

'I should speak to Muller,' said the captain, and he picked up the phone.

Returning to the top deck and Paula, Ben was surprised to see Gwen getting out of a police car on the river bank.

'She's back,' he exclaimed. 'That's odd. Not enough to hold her, perhaps.' He watched as she was escorted back onto the ship by Carl Muller. 'Hang on here,' he said to Paula. 'I'll be back in a minute.'

By the time he reached reception Gwen was already disappearing down the companionway with Tess tagging along behind. Carl Muller was watching reflectively, but looked up as Ben joined him. In answer to the lifted eyebrow, he said, 'Not enough to keep her in custody. Or to charge her. And with no sign of her husband's body, it seems likely he is our murderer and the most we can get her for is collusion. My superiors think that if we return her to the ship and keep an eye on her, we might find them meeting up somewhere. After all, he has no passport and possibly little money.'

'You know about her covering up for him, then?'

'We spoke to the cabin maid, yes. It does seem that way.'

Deflated, Ben said, 'You seem to have it all well in hand. I'll leave you to it.'

Chapter 11

The following day, there was a rousing cheer as the *Diamond* restarted her engines and the passengers complied with Tess's exhortation that they 'give it up' one more time for the captain and crew. The atmosphere was sensibly lighter as everyone returned to making their choices between an afternoon's visit to a Moselle valley winery or a bike ride through the hills to the castle they could see on the skyline. It didn't take Ben and Paula long to opt for the wine tour; but they and everyone else were surprised when Gwen joined them on the coach. No one really knew what to say, until the blunt Blake remarked,

'I'd've thought you'd be on your way back home by now.'

'No, why would I do that?' asked Gwen, hauling her bad knees along the gangway. 'We saved up over a long time for this trip. Gwyn wouldn't want me to miss anything.' She plumped down with a bump and a sigh onto the seat immediately behind the exit in the middle of the bus. 'Good.

I like to sit here,' she remarked to anyone listening. 'More leg room.'

Everyone else turned to face the front, as Paula remarked to Ben in an undertone, 'Obviously one of the "what I want is what the dead would have wanted" school of thinking.'

'Shush,' said Ben. 'She'll hear you.'

'Doubt it,' said Paula. 'I'm coming to realise that our put-upon little old lady has a good grasp of what she wants and hears only what she wants.'

At the vineyard, they were halfway through the presentation and wine tasting when there was an interruption at the door and voices became audible outside in the yard. Looking through the window, Ben saw the winery's old Labrador struggle to its feet to greet a stranger, accompanied by a familiar shape.

'Oh boy,' he muttered to Paula. 'I think this is about to get very interesting.'

Blake, across the tasting table, overheard and, following Ben's gaze, said, 'Strewth. Not again!'

Carl Muller appeared in the doorway and looked around.

'Everyone please remain in their seats,' he said. They all did, with one exception. At the back of the room Gwen Rees rose to her unsteady feet and started to reverse towards the emergency exit. In one hand she held her stick. With the other she picked up an unopened bottle from the table in front of her and brandished it.

'Oh no,' she hissed. 'Oh no you don't, boy. Not again.' And taking another step back, she found herself in the arms of a burly policeman standing behind her. Screaming and waving the bottle was of no avail. The wine was removed neatly from her grasp as Carl Muller said,

'As you say, not again.' And proceeded to arrest her.

The assembled company spilled out into the yard, tastings forgotten, as the screams and yells, still audible through the closed windows of the black van, disappeared towards the main road. Ben went up to Carl.

'You found the body,' he said. It wasn't a question.

'That's right,' said Carl with considerable satisfaction.

'And there's no doubt she did it.'

'None,' said Carl. 'The body had been in a Dutch mortuary for a day or so. A local investigation was already underway but they hadn't connected it with our problems. It was pulled out of the river two days ago, shortly after it went in, and therefore a long, long way downstream of where we began to look. You might be interested to know he was dressed in a towelling robe.'

'I think the cabin maid will be interested,' replied Ben. 'She's still furious about the suggestion she slipped up. Was it a blunt head trauma?'

'Yes, and no. There was one, and it was similar to the first victim. I think you were right, my friend. A champagne bottle seems very probable, but we may never find it. It probably went into the river.'

'Then how can you prove it was Gwen?'

'As I said, the body was retrieved from the river fairly, erm, fresh. He had been hit over the head, but that wasn't what killed him. The autopsy found another wound, partially hidden by the contusion from the bottle. A long thin wound deep into the brain. Such as would be caused by pushing

something long, sharp and narrow through his ear.'

Ben looked at him sharply. 'A hat pin,' he said.

'Precisely. Probably the hat pin Mrs Rees is so conveniently wearing today. It has been confiscated,' he added.

'Means and opportunity,' said Ben to himself. 'That's a wound you're only likely to get from someone you trust. Like a wife.'

'And therefore, why she went to such lengths to hide the wound and the body.'

'Motive?' asked Ben.

'At the moment we don't know for sure, but it seems likely to be good old-fashioned money. I won't be surprised if we find the poor, oppressed wife you described to me has taken out an insurance policy.'

'And the second missing towelling robe?'

'Again, we may never find it but we're still looking along the river banks. I would make the guess that Mrs Rees was wearing it when she wielded her alcoholic club, and it was covered in blood.'

'But Bentham? What about Richard Bentham?'

'That's the worst,' said Muller, moving towards his car. 'As far as we can see that was purely to lend credibility to her story that her husband went over the side in an accident involving a bridge. It was a smokescreen. That poor man was in the wrong place at the wrong time and died as a convenience, no more.

'Do you know what she said to me just now?'

'No. What?'

'When I said we'd be charging her with the murder of Richard Bentham as well, she shrugged and said, "Who cares? He won't be missed."'

A silence fell between them. Muller turned to leave, then turned back again.

'That poor, oppressed old lady you described to me. She may well have been badly treated by her husband. I could understand her taking revenge. But what she said about Richard Bentham!' He shrugged. 'For the first time in my career I felt I was in the presence of evil.'